Sunny

the Yellow
Fairy

Previously published as *Saffron the Yellow Fairy*

To the fairies at the
bottom of my garden

Special thanks to
Sue Bentley

No part of this publication may be reproduced in whole
or in part, or stored in a retrieval system, or transmitted
in any form or by any means, electronic, mechanical,
photocopying, recording, or otherwise, without written
permission of the publisher. For information regarding permission,
write to Working Partners Limited, 1 Albion Place, London,
W60QT, United Kingdom.

ISBN 0-439-74466-0

Copyright © 2003 by Working Partners Limited.
Illustrations copyright © 2003 by Georgie Ripper.

All rights reserved. Published by Scholastic Inc., 557 Broadway, New
York, NY 10012, by arrangement with Working Partners Limited.

SCHOLASTIC, LITTLE APPLE, and associated logos are trademarks
and/or registered trademarks of Scholastic Inc. Rainbow Magic is a
trademark of Working Partners Limited.

12 11 10 9 8 7 6 5 4   5 6 7 8 9 10/0

Printed in the U.S.A.

Sunny
the Yellow
Fairy

Previously published as *Saffron the Yellow Fairy*

by Daisy Meadows

illustrated by Georgie Ripper

A
LITTLE APPLE
PAPERBACK

SCHOLASTIC INC.

New York Toronto London Auckland Sydney
Mexico City New Delhi Hong Kong Buenos Aires

The
Fairyland
Palace

Maze

Forest

Orchard

Black
Pot

Meadow

Tower

Beach

Tide pools

Rainspell Island

Jack Frost's
Ice Castle

Tom Goodfellow's
House

Merry-go-round

Willow
Tree

Mrs. Merry's
Cottage

Stream

Field

Town

Mermaid
Cottage

Harbor

Dolphin Cottage

Cold winds blow and thick ice forms,
I conjure up this fairy storm.
To seven corners of the human world
the Rainbow Fairies will be hurled!

I curse every part of Fairyland,
with a frosty wave of my icy hand.
For now and always, from this day,
Fairyland will be cold and gray!

Ruby and Amber have been rescued.
Now it's time to search for
Sunny the Yellow Fairy!

Contents

A Very Big Bee

"Over here, Kirsty!" called Rachel Walker. Kirsty Tate ran across one of the emerald-green fields that covered this part of Rainspell Island. Buttercups and daisies dotted the grass.

"Don't go too far!" Kirsty's mom called. She and Kirsty's dad were climbing over a fence at the edge of the field.

Kirsty caught up with her friend.

"What did you find, Rachel? Is it another Rainbow Fairy?" she asked hopefully.

"I don't know." Rachel was standing on the bank of a rippling stream. "I thought I heard something."

Kirsty's face lit up. "Maybe there's a fairy in the stream?"

Rachel nodded. She knelt down on the soft grass and put her ear close to the water.

Kirsty crouched down, too, and listened really hard.

The sun glittered on the water as it splashed over big, shiny pebbles. Tiny rainbows flashed and sparkled — red, orange, yellow, green, blue, indigo, and violet.

And then the girls heard a tiny
bubbling voice. "Follow me. . . ." it
gurgled. "Follow me. . . ."

"Oh!" Rachel gasped. "Did you
hear that?"

"Yes," said Kirsty, her eyes wide. "It
must be a *magic* stream!"

Rachel felt her heart beat fast.

"Maybe the stream will lead us to the
Yellow Fairy," she said.

Rachel and Kirsty had a special secret. They had promised the King and Queen of Fairyland they would find the lost Rainbow Fairies. Jack Frost's spell had hidden the Rainbow Fairies on Rainspell Island. Fairyland would be cold and gray until all seven fairies had been found and returned to their home.

Silver fish darted in and out of the bright green weeds at the bottom of the stream. "Follow us, follow us. . . ." they whispered in tinkling voices.

Rachel and Kirsty smiled at each other. Titania, the Fairy Queen, had said that the magic would find them!

Kirsty's parents came up behind the girls and stopped to admire the stream, too. "Which way now?" asked Mr. Tate. "You two seem to know where you're going."

"Let's go this way," Kirsty said, pointing along the bank.

A brilliant bluebird flew up from its perch on a twig. Butterflies as bright as jewels fluttered among the cattails.

"Everything on Rainspell Island is so beautiful," said Kirsty's mom. "I'm glad we still have five days of vacation left!"

Yes, Rachel thought, *and five Rainbow Fairies still to find: Sunny, Fern, Sky, Inky, and Heather!* Ruby the Red Fairy and Amber the Orange Fairy were already safe in the pot at the end of the rainbow, thanks to Rachel and Kirsty.

The girls ran on ahead of Mr. and Mrs. Tate. As they followed the bubbling stream, the sun went behind a big, dark cloud.

A chilly breeze ruffled Kirsty's hair. She
noticed that some of the
leaves on the trees
were turning
brown, even
though it wasn't
autumn. Strange
weather like that
could only mean
one thing. "It looks
like Jack Frost's
goblins are still
around," she warned Rachel. Whenever
the goblins were nearby, everything
turned frosty and cold.

Rachel shivered. "Horrible creatures!
They'll do anything to stop the
Rainbow Fairies from getting back to
Fairyland."

The two friends stared anxiously up at the sky. But just then, the sun came out again, warming their shoulders. The girls smiled with relief and continued to follow the bubbling water.

The stream wound through a field covered with green clover. A herd of black-and-white cows was grazing at the water's edge. They looked up with their huge, brown eyes.

"Aren't they cute?" Kirsty asked.
Suddenly, the cows tossed their heads
and ran off toward the
other end of the field.
Rachel and Kirsty
looked at each other
in surprise. What was
going on?

Then they heard a loud
buzzing noise.

A small shape came
whizzing through the air, straight
toward them! Rachel jumped. "It's a
bee!" she gasped.

"Run!" Kirsty cried. "The cows had
the right idea!" Rachel tore through the
meadow with Kirsty right next to her,
their feet pounding the grass.

"Keep running, girls," called Mr. Tate,

catching up with them.
"That bee seems like it's
following us!"

Rachel glanced back
over her shoulder. The bee
was huge, bigger than
any bee she'd ever seen.

"In here, quick!" Mrs. Tate called
from the side of the field. She pulled
open a wooden gate.

They all ran through it, then stopped to catch their breath. Hopefully, they'd lost that bee — for good!

"I wonder who lives here," Kirsty panted. They were standing in a beautiful yard. A path led up to a little cottage with yellow roses around the door.

Just then, a very strange creature came out from behind some trees. It looked like an alien from outer space!

"Oh!" Rachel and Kirsty gasped.

The creature lifted its gloved hands and removed its white helmet to reveal . . . an  old woman! She smiled at them.

"Sorry if I scared you," she said. "I do look a little strange in my beekeeper's suit."

Rachel sighed in relief. It wasn't an alien after all!

"I'm Mrs. Merry," the old lady went on.

"Hello," Rachel said. "I'm Rachel. This is my friend Kirsty."

"And this is my mom and dad," Kirsty added. Mr. and Mrs. Tate greeted Mrs. Merry. Then Mr. Tate ducked as the huge bee zoomed past his ear. "Watch out!" he said. "It's back!"

"Oh, it's that hiveless queen again," said Mrs. Merry. She flapped her hand at the bee. "Go on, shoo!"

Rachel watched it swoop over a low hedge and disappear.

"That bee chased us all the way here. Why would she do that?" Kirsty asked.

"I don't think she was chasing you, my dear," said Mrs. Merry. "She was just heading this way because she's looking for a hive of her own. But all of my hives already have queens."

"Well, thank goodness she's gone now!" said Mrs. Tate.

"Since you're here, would you like to try some of my honey?" Mrs. Merry asked. Her blue eyes sparkled happily.

"Oh, yes, please," said Rachel.

The others nodded, and they followed

Mrs. Merry across the lawn to a table
covered with rows of jars.

Each jar was filled with
rich golden honey.
Rays of sunlight danced
over the jars, making
the honey glow.

"Here you
are," said Mrs.
Merry, spooning some honey onto a
pretty yellow plate.

"Thank you," Rachel said politely.
She dipped her finger into the little pool
of honey and popped it into her mouth.
The honey was the most delicious thing
she had ever tasted — sweet and smooth.

Then she felt it begin to tingle on her
tongue. She looked over at Kirsty. "It
tastes all fizzy!" she whispered.

Kirsty dipped her finger into the
honey, too. "And look!" she said.

Rachel saw that the honey was
twinkling with thousands of tiny, gold
sparkles. She grabbed Kirsty's arm. "Do
you think this means —"

"Yes," said Kirsty. Her eyes were
shining. "Another Rainbow Fairy must
be nearby!"

The Magic Hive

"We have to find out where this honey came from!" Rachel said excitedly.

"Yes," Kirsty agreed. "Mom? Can we stay here a bit longer, please?"

"As long as it's OK with Mrs. Merry," Kirsty's mom replied.

Mrs. Merry beamed. "Of course they can stay," she said kindly.

Mr. and Mrs. Tate decided to continue their walk. "Make sure you come back to Dolphin Cottage by lunchtime," Kirsty's mom said. "And be careful!"

"We will," Kirsty promised.

"Come along then, girls." Mrs. Merry set off across the smooth, green lawn.

Rachel and Kirsty followed her to some old and twisted apple trees. Six wooden hives stood underneath.

Kirsty stared at the row of hives. "Which one did the honey we tasted come from?" she asked.

Mrs. Merry looked pleased. "Did you enjoy it? The honey from that hive tastes especially good at the moment."

Rachel and Kirsty grinned at each other.

"I think we might know why," Rachel whispered to Kirsty.

"Yes," Kirsty agreed. "It could be fairy honey!"

"That's the one," Mrs. Merry said proudly, pointing to the very back of the yard. One hive stood there all alone, beneath the tallest apple tree.

As they walked toward the hive,
the girls could hear a sleepy
buzzing sound.
"The bees in this hive
are very peaceful
nowadays," said
Mrs. Merry.
"I've never known
them to be so happy."

"Can we get a bit closer?" Rachel
asked eagerly. She couldn't wait to find
out if the hive held a magical secret!

Mrs. Merry looked thoughtful. "I think
it's safe, with the bees so quiet," she
decided. "But you had better wear a
hood like mine, just in case."

She went into a nearby shed and
brought out two beekeepers' hoods.
"Here you are."

Rachel and Kirsty pulled the hoods over their heads. It was a bit dark and stuffy inside, but they could see through the netting just fine.

They moved closer to the hive. The soft buzzing sounded almost like music.

"We need to open it and take a look," Kirsty whispered to Rachel.

Rachel nodded.

But they couldn't start searching for the Yellow Fairy with Mrs. Merry there. Ruby had warned them that no grown-ups should see the fairies.

Suddenly, Kirsty had an idea. "Mrs. Merry, could I have a drink of water, please?" she asked.

"Of course you can, dear," Mrs. Merry said. "I'll be right back." She went off toward the cottage.

The girls waited until Mrs. Merry disappeared inside.

"Quick!" Kirsty spun around. "Let's open the hive."

Rachel grasped one end of the lid. Kirsty took hold of the other end. They pulled hard, and the lid slowly came loose with a squeaky sound. Strings of golden honey stretched down from it.

"Watch out. It's very sticky,"
Rachel said.

The girls bent down and laid the
heavy wooden top carefully on the
ground. Kirsty wiped her fingers on the
grass.

"Look!" Rachel whispered as she
stood up.

Kirsty turned to see, and gasped.

A shower of sparkling gold dust shot up out of the hive. It hung in a soft cloud, shimmering and dancing in the sunlight. Fairy dust!

Rachel leaned over and peered down into the hive. A tiny girl was sitting cross-legged on a piece of honeycomb, in the middle of a golden sea of honey.

A bee lay with its head in her lap while she combed its silky hair. Several other bees were waiting their turn, buzzing gently.

"Oh, Kirsty," Rachel whispered. "We've found another Rainbow Fairy!"

Bee Friends

Rachel and Kirsty took off their hoods and stared down into the hive with excitement.

The fairy had bright yellow hair. She wore a necklace of golden raindrops and lots of sparkly golden bracelets. Her T-shirt and shorts were the color of buttercups.

Her delicate wings sparkled with a thousand shimmering rainbows.

"Oh, thank you for finding me!" the fairy said in a tinkling voice. "I'm Sunny the Yellow Fairy."

Rachel and Kirsty introduced themselves. "We've met two of your sisters already — Ruby and Amber," Kirsty added. Sunny beamed happily. "You've found Ruby and Amber?" She stood up, gently pushing the bee away.

"Yes. They're safe in the pot at the end of the rainbow," Rachel said.

Sunny clapped her tiny hands. "I can't *wait* to see them again." Suddenly, she looked worried. "Have you seen any of Jack Frost's goblins near here?" she asked.

"No, not here," Kirsty said. "But there were some by the pot yesterday."

"We hid behind a bush until they went away," Rachel explained.

"Goblins are scary," Sunny said in a trembling voice. "I've been safe from them here in the hive, with my bee friends." Rachel felt very sorry for Sunny. "It's all right. King Oberon sent one of his frog footmen to look after you and your sisters." Sunny cheered up. "I've been really worried about finding my sisters. Jack Frost's magic is so cold and strong."

"It won't be long now," Kirsty said. "We are going to find Fern, Sky, Inky, and Heather, too, aren't we, Rachel?"

"Yes. We promised," Rachel agreed.

"Oh, thank you!" Sunny said. She
threw out her arms and gave a shake of
her sparkling wings.

Fairy dust rose into the air and drifted
down around Rachel and Kirsty. Where
it landed, bright yellow butterflies
appeared, with tiny fluttering wings.

A large bee crawled out of one of the
waxy openings in the honeycomb next
to Sunny.

"This is my new friend, Queenie," said Sunny. She put her arms around the bee's neck and kissed the top of her furry head.

Queenie buzzed softly.

"She says hello," said Sunny.

"Hello, Queenie," Kirsty and Rachel said together.

Sunny picked up her tiny comb and began to comb Queenie's shiny hair. Another bee buzzed angrily.

"Don't worry, Petal, I'll comb your hair next," Sunny said.

Rachel and Kirsty looked at each other in dismay.

"What if Sunny wants to stay with Queenie and the other bees?" Kirsty whispered.

"Sunny, you have to come with us!" Rachel burst out. "Or Fairyland will never get its colors back! It will take all seven of the Rainbow sisters to undo Jack Frost's spell."

Forgetful Fairy

"Yes, you're right! We have to break Jack Frost's spell!" Sunny cried. She jumped to her feet and picked up her wand.

Suddenly, an icy wind swept by. Something crunched under Kirsty's feet. There was a small patch of frost on the grass. Rachel shivered as something cold brushed against her cheek.

"A snowflake in summer? What's happening?" she cried.

"Jack Frost's goblins must be nearby," Kirsty said worriedly.

Sunny's tiny teeth chattered with cold. "Oh, no! If they find me, they will stop me from getting back to Fairyland!"

Kirsty looked at Rachel in alarm. "Quick, we have to go!"

Rachel leaned down and lifted the fairy out of the beehive. Sunny's golden hair dripped with honey.

"Oh, my, you're really sticky!" Rachel said.

Just then, Kirsty spotted Mrs. Merry coming out of her cottage.

"I forgot I asked for a drink," Kirsty said. "What are we going to do about Sunny?"

Rachel thought for a moment, then dropped the fairy into the pocket of her shorts.

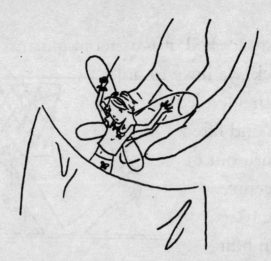

Sunny gave a cry of dismay. "Hey! It's dark in here!" she complained.

"Sorry," Rachel whispered. "I'll get you out again in a minute, I promise."

Suddenly, Kirsty noticed the open hive. "We have to put the top back on before Mrs. Merry sees it!" she said.

She bent down and grabbed the lid. Rachel helped lift it and they quickly put it into place, just as Mrs. Merry came through the trees.

"Here's your drink, dear," said Mrs. Merry, holding out a glass to Kirsty. She had taken off her strange suit, and was carrying a shopping basket in her other hand.

"Thank you very much," Kirsty said, taking the glass.

"Now, you girls stay as long as you like," said Mrs. Merry. "I must run out and buy some fish for my cat. It's time for his lunch!"

Rachel watched Mrs. Merry walk toward the garden gate. Then she slipped her hand into her pocket.

"You can come out now," she said to
Sunny, gently lifting her out.

The fairy was covered with gray fuzz
from Rachel's pocket. "Achoo!" Sunny
sneezed and brushed angrily at the bits
of sticky fuzz clinging to her wings. "I'm
all clogged up!" she wailed. "I won't be
able to fly."

"We can help clean you up," Rachel
said. "But we'll have to be quick, in case
the goblins find us."

Kirsty looked around and pointed to a stone birdbath filled with clear water. "Over there!"

"Just what we need," Rachel agreed. She carried Sunny over to the birdbath.

Sunny fluttered onto the edge of the bath, put down her wand, and dived in.

Splash!

The water fizzed and turned bright yellow. Lemony-smelling drops sprayed up into the air.

Sunny swam two circles, and before long she was sparkling clean. She zoomed up into the air to dry. Misty yellow trails appeared as she whooshed around. "That's better!" she cried.

She hovered in the air in front of Kirsty. Her wings flashed like gold in the sun. Then she swooped down onto Rachel's shoulder. "Come on, let's go to the pot at the end of the rainbow! I can't wait to see my sisters!"

Rachel nodded. She wanted to leave the garden before the goblins got there.

"Good-bye, Queenie!" Sunny called, waving to her friend. "I'll come back to visit as soon as I can!"

Queenie peeked out of the hive. She seemed a bit sad that Sunny was

leaving. Her feelers drooped as she
waved a tiny leg and buzzed good-bye.

Sunny sat cross-legged on Rachel's
shoulder as they headed for the woods.
Suddenly, she cried out and flew up into
the air. "Oh, no!" She gasped. "I left my
wand next to the birdbath!"

Rachel looked at Kirsty with concern.
"We'll have to go back," she said.

"Yes," Kirsty agreed. "We can't leave a fairy wand lying around for the goblins to find."

"Oh, dear . . . Oh, dear . . ." Sunny zipped back and forth, wringing her hands as they headed back down the path.

Rachel paused at the gate and looked into the garden. There was no sign of goblins.

Kirsty and Rachel ran through the apple trees, toward the birdbath. Sunny fluttered just above them.

Suddenly, an icy blast made them all shiver. They gazed around in alarm. Icicles now hung from the apple trees, and the whole lawn was white and crunchy with frost. The goblins had arrived! And they'd brought winter to the lovely garden.

Sunny gave a cry of horror.

An ugly, hook-nosed goblin jumped up on top of Queenie's hive. His bulging eyes gleamed. In one hand he was holding Sunny's wand!

Well Done, Queenie

"Give me back my wand!"
Sunny demanded.

"Come and get it!"
yelled the goblin rudely.
He leaped off the hive and
ran toward the gate.

Kirsty gasped as another goblin
jumped down from the apple tree.

Crunch! He landed on the frosty grass
and set off at a run.

"Catch!" The goblin threw the wand
to his friend. It flew through the air,
shooting out yellow sparks.

The other goblin reached up and
caught the wand. "Hee, hee. Got it!"

"Oh, no!" Sunny gasped.

Just then, Queenie flew out of the
hive with a loud buzz. All the other
bees swarmed behind her in a noisy
cloud.

Rachel watched, her eyes very wide.
With Queenie in the lead, the bees
formed into an arrow shape and raced
after the goblins.

"Be careful, Queenie!" pleaded Sunny.

"Get away!" The goblin shook Sunny's wand at Queenie.

More bright yellow sparks shot out of the wand. One of the sparks hit Queenie's wing. Queenie wobbled in midair. Then she buzzed angrily and flew at the goblin again.

buzzzzzz

"Help!" The goblin ducked and dropped the wand.

"Butterfingers!" grumbled the other goblin, scooping it up and continuing to run.

"They're getting
away!" Kirsty cried.

Queenie and her
bees rose into
the air again.

"No, they're
not!" Rachel cried
excitedly. The bees shot across the yard
and the goblins disappeared in the
angry swarm.

"Get off me!" sputtered the goblin
with the wand. He
tried to shoo the bees
away, but tripped
over his own
feet. As he fell,
he bumped
into the other
goblin.

The two of them tumbled over in a
heap, dropping the wand onto the grass.

"That was your fault!" complained
one of the goblins.

"No, it wasn't!" snapped the other one.

Queenie zoomed over and picked up
the wand with one of her tiny, black feet.

She carried it straight to Sunny,
who was standing on Rachel's hand.
With a little buzz, Queenie landed next
to Sunny.

Sunny took her wand from Queenie and carefully waved it in the air. A fountain of glittering dust and fluttering butterflies sparkled around them. "My wand is all right!" Sunny cried joyfully. "Look! The goblins are leaving," Kirsty said. The rest of the bees had chased the goblins to the edge of the yard. Still arguing, the goblins ran across the fields.

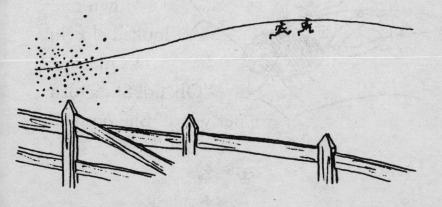

As the grumbling voices faded away, the icy wind disappeared. The sun shone warmly again and the frost melted. The bees streamed back and flew around Rachel and Kirsty, buzzing softly.

"Thank you, Queenie!" Sunny's eyes sparkled as she hugged her friend.

Suddenly, Queenie wobbled and tipped sideways.

Rachel cupped her hands, worried that Queenie would roll off. "I think she might be hurt," she said. Sunny knelt down and looked closely at Queenie. "Oh, no! She's torn her wing!" She gasped.

"It must have happened when she fought the goblin," Rachel said.

"Can you heal Queenie's wing with magic?" Kirsty asked Sunny.

Sunny shook her head. "Not on my own. But Amber or Ruby might be able to help me. We have to take Queenie to the pot at the end of the rainbow right away!"

Fairy Repairs

Rachel and Kirsty hurried across the fields and into the woods. Rachel carefully held Queenie in her cupped hands, while Sunny flew behind them, her rainbow-colored wings shimmering in the sun.

"There's the willow tree where the pot is hidden," Kirsty said. She went

over and parted the branches, which
hung right down to the ground. The
black pot lay on its side in the grass. A
large, green frog hopped out from
behind it.

"Bertram!" Sunny flew down and
hugged him. "I'm so glad you're here!"

Bertram bowed his head. "It's a pleasure, Miss Sunny," he said. "Miss Ruby and Miss Amber will be delighted to see you."

Suddenly, a shower of red and orange fairy dust shot up out of the pot, followed by Ruby and Amber.

"Sunny!" Ruby shouted. "It really *is* you!"

"It's so good to have you back!" Amber called happily. Kirsty and Rachel smiled as the fairies hugged and kissed one another.

The air around them fizzed with red
flowers, orange bubbles, and tiny,
yellow butterflies.

Ruby flew onto Kirsty's shoulder.
"Thank you, Rachel and Kirsty," she
said. "Now three of us are safe." Then
she spotted Queenie lying on Rachel's
hand. "Who is this?" she asked.

"This is my friend Queenie," Sunny explained. "She helped me get my wand back after the goblins stole it."

"Goblins?" Ruby shuddered. "You were very brave to fight them, Queenie." She flew down and stroked Queenie's head.

"One of the goblins used my wand to hurt Queenie's wing. Can you help her?" Sunny asked her sisters.

Amber thought hard. "I could mend Queenie's wing if I had a fairy needle and thread," she said. Then she looked sad. "But I don't have any here in the pot."

Then Rachel remembered something. "Kirsty! What about the magic bags that the Fairy Queen gave us?"

"Oh, yes," Kirsty said. She reached into her pocket and pulled out her bag. It was glowing with a soft, silver light.

When she opened it, a cloud of glitter shot up into the air. Kirsty slipped her hand into the bag. "There's something here." She drew out a tiny, shining needle, threaded with fine spider silk. She held it out to Amber.

"Perfect!" Amber said. She flew onto Rachel's hand and sat next to Queenie.

Amber stroked Queenie's black-and-yellow head. "Don't worry," she said. "It's fairy magic, so it won't hurt."

Kirsty watched as Amber carefully wove the needle in and out of the torn wing. The row of stitches glowed like tiny silver dots.

"Look, they're starting to fade," Rachel said.

"Yes," said Amber. "When you can't see them anymore, the wing will be healed."

Queenie buzzed softly. She lifted her
head and flapped her wings. Then she
zoomed into the air. Her
wing was as good as new!
She swooped down and
landed next to
Amber. Bowing her
head, she rubbed
her feelers against
the fairy's hand.
"You have been
such a good friend
to Sunny, you
have to stay with
us," said Amber,
hugging the bee.
"Yes!" Ruby agreed. "Please
come and stay with us, just
until we go back to Fairyland."

Queenie flew over to Sunny and
buzzed in her ear.

"She says she would love to," said
Sunny. "There is a hiveless queen in
Mrs. Merry's yard who would be happy
to take care of her bees. Come on,
Queenie. Let's look at our new home."

"Let's take a look, too," Kirsty said.
Rachel crouched down beside her in
the grass. They watched the
fairy sisters and the queen bee
fly into the pot.

Sunny beamed when
she saw all the tiny
furniture. She sat down
on a soft, mossy cushion.
"This is just like our
home in Fairyland," she
said. Then her face fell.

"But what about the rest of our sisters? They are still trapped somewhere on the island!"

"Don't worry," Kirsty said. "We'll find them soon."

"Yes, we will," Rachel agreed, jumping up. She looked at her watch. "It's almost lunchtime. We have to go. But we'll see you again very soon."

The fairies looked up and waved.

"Good-bye! Good-bye!" Queenie waved a tiny leg and buzzed.

Bertram, the frog footman, followed the girls out from under the willow tree. "Ruby, Amber, and Sunny will be safe here with me," he said. "But you have to be careful when you go looking for the others. Watch out for goblins!"

"We will," Rachel promised.

Kirsty looked back at the pot at the end of the rainbow. "Nothing will stop us from finding the other Rainbow Fairies!" she said.

Ruby, Amber, and Sunny are
out of danger. Now Rachel
and Kirsty need to find

Fern the Green Fairy!

Will they find her in time?
Join Kirsty and Rachel's adventure in
this special sneak peek. . . .

A Secret Garden

"Oh!" Rachel Walker gasped in delight as she looked around her. "What a perfect place for a picnic!"

"It's a secret garden," Kirsty Tate said, her eyes shining.

The two girls were standing in a large garden. It looked as if nobody else had been there for a long, long time.

Pink and white roses grew all around the tree trunks, filling the air with their sweet smell. White marble statues stood here and there, half hidden by green ivy. And right in the middle of the garden was a crumbling stone tower.

"There was a castle here once called Moonspinner Castle," Mr. Walker said, walking up behind them and looking at his guidebook. "But now all that's left is the tower."

Rachel and Kirsty stared up at the ruined tower. The yellow stones glowed warmly in the sunshine. They were spotted with soft, green moss. Near the top of the tower was a small, square window.

"It's just like Rapunzel's tower," Kirsty said. "I wonder if we can get up to the top somehow."

"Let's go see!" Rachel said eagerly. "I want to explore the whole garden. Can we, Mom?"

"Go ahead." Mrs. Walker smiled. "Your dad and I will get the food ready." She opened the picnic basket. "But don't be too long, girls."

Rachel and Kirsty rushed over to the door in the side of the tower.

Read the rest of

RAINBOW magic

Fern the Green Fairy
to find out what Rachel and Kirsty discover at the top of the tower.

Help Find Fern the Green Fairy!

In Stores September 2005

Rainbow Magic #4: Fern the Green Fairy • 0-439-744-679
by Daisy Meadows

Join Rachel and Kirsty on the search for Fern the Green Fairy. She's trappped in a secret garden maze and can't find her way out! Can Rachel and Kirsty help Fern get back to the pot at the end of the rainbow?

www.scholastic.com

SCHOLASTIC